ALIEN INVADERS

ALIEN INVADERS: ZILLAH, THE FANGED PREDATOR
A RED FOX BOOK 978 1 849 41232 2

First published in Great Britain by Red Fox,
an imprint of Random House Children's Books
A Random House Group Company

This edition published 2011

1 3 5 7 9 10 8 6 4 2

The Random House Group Limited supports the Forest Stewardship
Council® (FSC®), the leading international forest certification organisation.
All our titles that are printed on Greenpeace approved FSC® certified paper
carry the FSC® logo. Our paper procurement policy can be found at
www.randomhouse.co.uk/environment

MIX
Paper from
responsible sources
FSC® C016897

Set in Century Schoolbook

Red Fox Books are published by Random House Children's Books,
61–63 Uxbridge Road, London W5 5SA

www.kidsatrandomhouse.co.uk
www.randomhouse.co.uk

Addresses for companies within The Random House Group Limited can be
found at: www.randomhouse.co.uk/offices.htm

THE RANDOM HOUSE GROUP Limited Reg. No. 954009

A CIP catalogue record for this book is available from
the British Library.

Printed and bound in Great Britain by CPI Bookmarque,
Croydon, CR0 4TD

ALIEN INVADERS

MAX SILVER

ZILLAH
THE FANGED PREDATOR

RED FOX

THE GALAXY

PLANET ZAMAN

TARN BELT

DELTA QUADRANT

GAMMA QUADRANT

PLANET ABU

PLANET OCEANIA

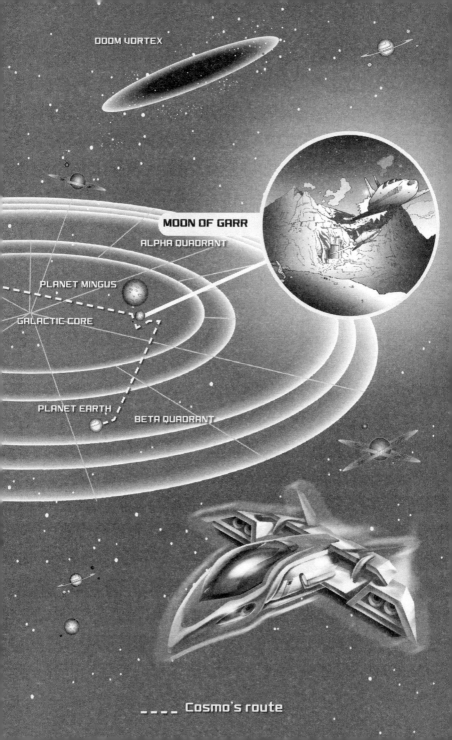

DOOM VORTEX

MOON OF GARR

ALPHA QUADRANT

PLANET MINGUS

GALACTIC CORE

PLANET EARTH

BETA QUADRANT

_ _ _ _ Cosmo's route

ATTENTION, ALL EARTHLINGS!

MY NAME IS G1 AND I AM CHIEF OF THE GALAXY'S SECURITY FORCE, G-WATCH. I BRING YOU GRAVE NEWS.

IT IS THE YEAR 2121, AND OUR PLANETS ARE UNDER ATTACK FROM THE OUTLAW KAOS. HE IS BEAMING FIVE ALIEN INVADERS INTO THE GALAXY, COMMANDING THEM TO DESTROY IT. IF THEY SUCCEED, THIS WILL BE THE END OF US ALL.

A HERO MUST BE FOUND TO SAVE US: ONE WHO WILL VENTURE THROUGH THE TREACHEROUS REGIONS OF SPACE; ONE WITH AN UNCOMMON COURAGE WITH WHICH TO FIGHT THESE INVADERS; ONE WHO POSSESSES THE POWER OF THE UNIVERSE! THAT HERO IS AN EARTHLING BOY. HE IS OUR ONLY HOPE.

INVADER ALERT!

Aboard space station *Orpheus*, Captain Provix kept watch as a convoy of eight cargo freighters approached along the Great Western Tradeway. The freighters were heading towards a vast zone of swirling asteroids: the Tarn Asteroid Belt. Provix reached out his webbed hand, switching on the space station's communicator. "*Orpheus* to convoy. I have a visual on you. Please reduce engine speed now."

"Instruction received," came the reply. "This is Convoy Leader Fortuna. How are conditions today? Are we in for a bumpy ride?"

Captain Provix pressed a sequence of buttons on the space station's control desk, activating its satellite receivers and deep-space imaging equipment. "The Tarn Asteroid Belt is experiencing erratic storms," he replied. "But *Orpheus* will guide you safely through. Sit back and relax. I'm locking on to you now."

The station's transmitters whirred as its supercomputer took control of the freighters' navigation consoles, overriding them and reprogramming their course.

Space station *Orpheus* was an advanced navigation station that monitored conditions in the Tarn Asteroid Belt, a wild zone of swirling rocks, debris and space dust that intersected the Great Western Tradeway. The area was a major danger to freighters trying to make essential galactic deliveries, and only *Orpheus* could guide them safely through.

Captain Provix had worked on *Orpheus* for six Tarn years. He was an experienced navigator from the distant planet Pialor, and his solitary temperament was well-suited to long periods spent alone in deep space. He watched from the control room as *Orpheus* remotely steered the eight freighters safely between moving asteroids, directing them on their journey through the Tarn Belt. He entered the convoy's details into the computer's log:

```
CONVOY: 10786956
COMPRISED OF: 8 DUCANOID FREIGHTERS
CARGO: GRAIN
DESTINATION: WESTERN WORL—
```

Suddenly the space station shuddered, throwing Captain Provix to the floor. *What was that – an asteroid hit?* he thought.

The emergency alarm sounded: *Whoop! Whoop! Whoop!*

Provix grabbed hold of the control desk, pulling himself up. Through the lookout sphere he saw *Orpheus*'s satellite dishes, antennae and probes spinning off into space. Warning lights were flashing on the control desk and the space station was rocking violently. Quickly he switched on the communicator. "Mayday! Mayday! This is Captain Provix requesting urgent help. Space station *Orpheus* is in trouble!"

He waited for a reply, but none came; the station's transmitters were down too. He heard a clawing and scratching sound coming from outside. *Something's attacking* Orpheus*!* he realized in terror.

Provix heard the station's metal hull being torn and wrenched apart. Suddenly there was a shrill hiss, and two long fangs pierced through the ceiling of the control room. Provix gasped. Green slime began oozing down the fangs, dripping onto the desk. It was some kind of chemical and

the desk started to fizz and bubble,
dissolving *Orpheus*'s supercomputer!

Captain Provix cowered, clinging to the
control panel as the metal ceiling tore open
and a hideous face looked in – the face of
a huge fanged alien with jet-black eyes.

"I am ZZZZZillah," the alien hissed.
"And in the name of Kaosss I come to feed!"

CHAPTER ONE

TRADEWAY TROUBLE

"Hey, Nuri, what are you doing back there?" Cosmo called, as he blasted the Dragster 7000 spaceship away from the Dyad-24 star system, heading for the galaxy's Great Western Tradeway.

Agent Nuri, his blue-skinned co-pilot from Planet Etrusia, entered through the cockpit's interior door. "I've brought you something to eat," she said, handing him a pot of pink paste.

Cosmo looked at it, puzzled. "What is it?"

"It's space food from the supply cupboard," she told him.

"It looks revolting," Cosmo said, wrinkling his nose.

Brain-E, the ship's brainbot, bleeped from the Dragster's control desk and dipped its probe arm into the paste. "Master Cosmo, this contains precisely two thousand calories, plus protein, minerals and vitamins A, B, C, D, E, K and P. It's been specially designed in the G-Watch laboratory for deep-space missions."

Cosmo scooped out a blob of the pink paste and swallowed it. "Mmmm, it's not bad," he said, surprised. It tasted like strawberry ice cream. He tucked in hungrily as the Dragster 7000 powered onwards, knowing he had to keep his strength up for what lay ahead.

Cosmo was an eleven-year-old Earthling boy on an urgent mission for the galaxy's security force, G-Watch. The evil outlaw, Kaos, had five fearsome alien invaders under his command, and was sending them to destroy the galaxy. Only Cosmo could protect it from their attack. Already he'd defeated two of them: Rockhead, the living mountain, and Infernox, the firestarter. Now he was trying to locate and fight the third invader: Zillah, the fanged predator.

"Nuri, could you select our course?" Cosmo asked.

"Right away," Nuri replied, programming the spaceship's navigation console. Details appeared on the spacescreen.

```
DESTINATION: GREAT WESTERN TRADEWAY,
TARN JUNCTION
STAR SYSTEM: TARN ASTEROID BELT
ROUTE: HYPERWAY 7 JOINING TRADEWAY AT JUNCTION L2
DISTANCE: 2 BILLION MILES
```

Having eaten, Cosmo felt ready for adventure. He'd been recruited secretly for this mission because of the unique power inside him – a lightning-like energy that gave him courage in the face of danger and activated the special spacesuit he was wearing, called the Quantum Mutation Suit. It was G-Watch's most advanced piece of technology, made from a living fabric that allowed Cosmo to mutate into different alien forms to fight any opponent.

He shot the Dragster between flashing space beacons onto Hyperway 7 then flicked the Dragster's hyperdrive switch; the stars on the spacescreen turned to bright streaks as he accelerated to twice the speed of light.

Nuri checked the course. "In two Earth minutes we'll reach Junction L2 of the Great Western Tradeway."

"What is this tradeway, anyway?" Cosmo asked.

"It's an essential route for spaceships travelling through the galaxy's Delta Quadrant," Nuri explained. "All kinds of freighters use it to trade supplies between the planets."

And now there's a fearsome alien on it, Cosmo thought. *Not good*. As they approached Junction L2, he switched out of hyperdrive and veered onto the Great Western Tradeway. He swerved to pass a slow-moving cargo ship then zipped by a line of livestock transporters. The tradeway was busy with space traffic; there were high-security ships transporting galactic gold and thick-hulled freighter vessels carrying food supplies.

Nuri glanced up from the navigation console. "G-Watch's scanners detected the invader beaming in near the Tarn Junction, where the tradeway enters the Tarn Asteroid Belt."

"Brain-E, what do you know about this invader?" Cosmo asked.

The ship's brainbot bleeped. "Well, according to my databank, Zillah is a female predator from the Doom Vortex; a scavenger who feeds on space wreckage in the vortex's treacherous storm zones."

"A scavenger that eats spaceships!" Cosmo said, shocked. "I don't want to end up as some freaky alien's lunch."

"Cosmo, slow down!" Nuri said.

Ahead of them was a space traffic jam: hundreds of ships were stuck on the tradeway. Cosmo reduced power. *What's going on?* he wondered. He weaved the Dragster between the ships, trying to find out. They were bottle-necked on the edge of a vast mass of swirling asteroids. On the spacescreen, the star plotter lit up, highlighting the asteroids, and a flashing red message appeared: DANGER! TARN ASTEROID BELT! DO NOT ENTER!

"This is weird," Nuri commented. "*Orpheus* should be guiding these ships through. There shouldn't be any jam."

"What's *Orpheus*?" Cosmo asked, flying carefully between two cargo carriers.

"It's a navigation station. It should be close by."

Cosmo peered nervously through the spacescreen sensing that something was wrong. "Nuri, over there!" he said, spotting a mangled silver structure floating on the edge of the asteroid belt. "Is that *Orpheus*?"

Nuri looked to where Cosmo was pointing. "Yes! What's happened to it?"

Cosmo steered towards the space station, shining the Dragster's searchlights. *Orpheus* looked broken and twisted. The bent remains of antennae and satellites were hanging off it.

"It's been attacked," Cosmo said. "Zillah must have struck already!"

The beam of the Dragster's searchlights illuminated someone floating in *Orpheus*'s control room – a wolf-headed man wearing an emergency oxygen mask.

"Look, someone's inside," Cosmo said. "And he's in trouble. He needs our help!"

CHAPTER TWO

"IT'S BREAKING UP!"

Cosmo pulled up alongside *Orpheus*, attaching the Dragster to its docking magnets with a *clunk*. Pieces of metal were peeling off, drifting past the spacescreen.

"The space station's hull is breaking up. We'd better hurry," Nuri said, taking two white oxygen pills from her utility belt. "Swallow one of these, Cosmo. There'll be hardly any oxygen left inside."

Cosmo popped the pill into his mouth and felt it fizz. He grabbed a plasma torch from the kit shelf, then lifted the airlock hatch in the cockpit floor. "Brain-E, stay here and keep the engines running in case we need to make a quick getaway."

The brainbot flashed its lights. "Good luck!"

Cosmo stepped down through the hatch with Nuri following. She closed it behind them and Cosmo opened the airlock's outer hatch, pulling himself aboard *Orpheus*. The space station's power was down and it had lost gravity. Cosmo and Nuri floated down a dark metal corridor, shining their plasma torches ahead of them.

Cosmo heard clanging sounds from the control room at the end of the corridor. He prised open its door and shone his torch inside. It was drenched in green slime and there was a huge hole in the ceiling where a metal panel had been torn off.

The light from Cosmo and Nuri's torches revealed the wolf-headed man in the oxygen mask. He was trying desperately to fix the melting control desk. His eyes looked wild with fright.

"We're from G-Watch," Cosmo said. "We've come to help you."

"Oh, thank goodness," the man replied, his voice sounding muffled beneath the mask. "My name is Provix, and I'm *Orpheus*'s captain. The space station was attacked by a monster – some kind of enormous fanged alien."

"That alien's called Zillah," Cosmo explained.

"It tore *Orpheus* apart and injected green slime into the hull. It's dissolving the supercomputer!"

Nuri shone her plasma torch on the control desk and examined the green liquid. "This looks like some kind of acidic saliva capable of digesting metal," she said.

"You have to help me get the supercomputer working again," Captain Provix said desperately. "There's a convoy of eight cargo freighters travelling through the Tarn Belt right now. Without *Orpheus*'s navigation system to guide them, they'll never make it past the asteroids."

Cosmo could see the control desk bubbling and dissolving before his very eyes. He glanced at Nuri gravely, who shook her head.

"It's no use," she said. "We'd need new parts to fix the computer."

"Captain Provix, where did the alien go?" Cosmo asked.

"It went into the Tarn Belt too," Provix replied. "It fired a cable to an asteroid and swung away on it."

"A cable?"

"A white cable, like a spider's thread."

A loud creaking noise came from the ship's hull as the last rivets that were holding it together began to pop out.

"Captain Provix, we have to get you out of here," Cosmo said. "This place is breaking up. Does *Orpheus* have an escape pod?"

"Yes, it's back down the corridor,"
Provix said. "But what about the
freighters?"

"Nuri and I will go after the freighters,
Captain – and the alien too. Now, let's go!"

Cosmo pulled Captain Provix out of the
control room and down the dark corridor,
floating in zero gravity. Nuri shone her
torch on the hatch to the escape pod.

Cosmo opened it and helped the captain into a small torpedo-like capsule.

"Thank you," Provix said. "Good luck."

Cosmo closed the hatch. Instantly the pod fired away from the stricken space station onto the Great Western Tradeway, the force of its blast causing the corridor to shudder. There was a wrenching sound of metal and Cosmo felt the walls trembling. "Quick, Nuri, back to the Dragster!"

The corridor was collapsing around them as they pulled themselves along. They clambered through the Dragster's hatch, then burst back up into the cockpit.

"Brain-E, thrusters on!" Cosmo yelled.

The brainbot fired up the Dragster, and Cosmo jumped into the pilot's seat, blasting them away from the space station as it split apart. Fragments of metal and glass went spinning away through space.

"That was close," Cosmo said.

"Way too close," Nuri added, brushing green slime from her spacesuit sleeve.

"Nuri, could you radio G-Watch headquarters and inform them that all tradeway traffic is to stay out of the Tarn Asteroid Belt until instructed otherwise?"

"Right away," Nuri replied, reaching for the ship's communicator.

Brain-E bleeped. "But with the Tradeway at a standstill, the whole of the galaxy will suffer, Master Cosmo. Supplies won't get through and food will quickly run out."

Cosmo glanced at the space traffic jam. *That's why Kaos beamed Zillah here*, he thought. *We have to stop her!*

He looked towards the Tarn Belt, its asteroids swirling menacingly. "Zillah's in there somewhere, Nuri, and so is the convoy of freighters."

"They're in danger," Nuri replied.

Cosmo accelerated towards the vast swirling mass, and the warning flashed on the screen once more: DANGER! TARN ASTEROID BELT! DO NOT ENTER!

Brain-E's bug-like eyes extended on metal stalks, peering nervously out through the spacescreen. "Master Cosmo, you're not going to fly into the Tarn Belt unguided, are you? If those asteroids collide with the Dragster, they'll split us open like a tin can."

"We have no choice, Brain-E," Cosmo replied, tapping the spacescreen and

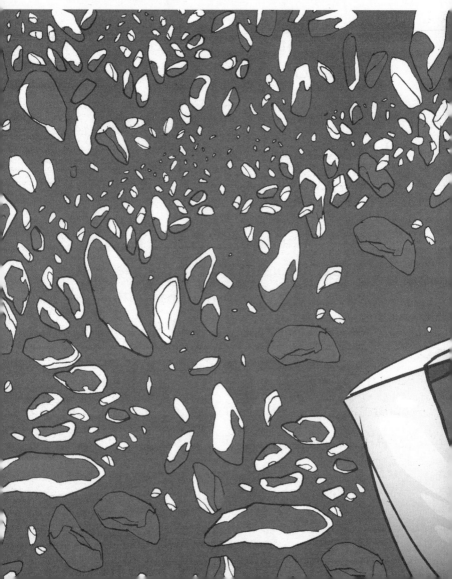

switching off the star plotter's warning.
He scanned his instruments, making
sure he was ready. "Hold on tight. We're
going in!"

CHAPTER THREE

ASTEROID ALERT!

Cosmo entered the Tarn Belt, flying the Dragster between two enormous asteroids. Nuri and Brain-E fell silent, their nerves on edge. Cosmo knew from his Space Studies lessons back at school on Earth that asteroid belts were some of the most dangerous regions in space, but nothing could have prepared him for this.

There was no starlight at all, and out of the darkness huge black lumps of rock were appearing one after another in the beams of the Dragster's searchlights. All around he could hear the muffled booming sounds of asteroids colliding. He tried to weave his way through them, but gusts of silent space wind buffeted the spaceship, causing it to veer off course.

An asteroid spun towards the ship, and he quickly plunged the Dragster into a nosedive, just managing to zoom beneath it. Space dust and particles of rock clattered against the spacescreen.

"Easy does it," Nuri said shakily, clutching the edge of her seat.

Cosmo continued through the darkness. His reactions were quick. "Nuri, we should try to contact the convoy of freighters and warn them about Zillah," he said.

"Good thinking," Nuri replied. She pressed a button on the ship's communicator, but heard only a crackle. "There's no signal."

Brain-E bleeped. "These asteroids will be causing electromagnetic interference."

Nuri searched through the different frequencies. "G-Watch to convoy. I repeat: this is G-Watch to convoy. Convoy, can you hear me?"

There was no reply.

"Keep trying," Cosmo said.

Some of the asteroids were the size of boulders; others must have been up to a hundred miles wide, big enough to crush a city. The Dragster's searchlights illuminated one with trees growing on it, and another with a snow-capped mountain peak. *This place is freaky*, Cosmo thought, swerving to avoid them. He saw a vast mass of glittering black ice spinning towards the ship, and swooped beneath it. The ice was the size of a frozen lake, with alien fish frozen inside it.

"Brain-E, what's ice doing here?" he asked, looking up through the spacescreen.

Brain-E bleeped. "That's the frozen lake of Planet Vaspa," it replied. "The Tarn Belt was once a giant solar system of twenty-seven planets that orbited the star Junol. About a thousand years ago, Junol exploded and the planets were blown to pieces. The asteroids here are the remnants of those planets."

The Dragster was approaching a cloud of blue sand.

"The ancient sand dunes of Planet Duro," Brain-E explained.

Cosmo reduced his speed, the blue sand smothering the spacescreen. He flew steadily through it and emerged into the path of more asteroids, some with extinct volcanoes, frozen rivers and even the ruins of a town. He banked and weaved, passing between them. *If I ever make it back to Earth alive, I'll be sure to tell my Space Studies class about this*, he thought.

"Still no reply," Nuri said, scanning the crackling airwaves, trying to contact the convoy.

"Keep a lookout for Zillah," Cosmo told her.

Nuri and Brain-E peered out either side of the spacescreen as Cosmo flew the ship onwards. As well as asteroids, its searchlights lit up several old space wrecks: a rocket's nose-cone, the tail-fin of a galactic ferry, and a battered container unit from an oil transporter.

"The Tarn Asteroid Belt used to be known as the spaceships' graveyard," Brain-E said. "Before *Orpheus* existed, there were many accidents here."

The sight of the pulverized ships didn't help Cosmo's confidence. Without *Orpheus*'s supercomputer to navigate the Dragster through safely, he had only his wits and courage to guide him.

"I think I heard something," Nuri said, leaning in to the crackling communicator, her pointy ears twitching.

Cosmo listened too. He could make out faint voices beneath the static:

"It's got me! Get out of here now!"

"I can't. It's biting my ship!"

"It's two pilots from the freighter convoy," Nuri said. "It sounds like they're being attacked!" She turned up the volume slightly. "This is the Dragster 7000 from G-Watch. Convoy, can you hear me? Please state your location."

But there was no reply, only more crackling. She tried adjusting the frequency but the signal had gone.

Cosmo frowned. "We've got to find them – *fast*."

"Master Cosmo, I'm afraid we have troubles of our own," Brain-E said, pointing to the needles on the Dragster's control desk. They were flickering wildly and lights were flashing too. "There's a space storm approaching."

Rocks and lumps of ice smashed against the spacescreen and a sudden gust of turbulence hurled the Dragster sideways. Electromagnetic lightning bolts flashed up ahead and Cosmo heard asteroids colliding. *Uh-oh*, he thought. *I don't like the look of this!*

The Dragster began to roll and dip as the wind picked up.

"Watch out!" Nuri said, as a huge rock spun towards them.

Cosmo swerved the Dragster just in time.

"Master Cosmo, flying through an asteroid field during a space storm is suicide," Brain-E said, cowering on the control desk. "We should turn back."

"We can't. We have to find Zillah and rescue those freighter pilots," Cosmo replied. The storm was almost upon them now, tossing the Dragster up and down. Cosmo tightened his safety harness and gripped the steering column with determination. "I'm going to have to fly us through it."

CHAPTER FOUR

SPACE STORM!

"Incoming!" Nuri yelled as a massive asteroid spun towards them.

Cosmo pulled on the steering column and soared above it. But as he did so, another asteroid hurtled towards the spaceship from the right. He swerved to avoid it, but flew into the path of two more asteroids the size of mountains. The Dragster shot between them, making it through as they collided with a *boom!*

"Watch out, Cosmo!" Nuri called as the battered wreck of an old space plough came spinning towards them. Cosmo quickly banked the Dragster, twisting sideways. With a sickening screech of metal, the space plough scraped against the Dragster's hull. An alarm sounded in the cockpit – *Whoop! Whoop! Whoop!* – and a red warning light flashed, signalling that the ship was damaged. Cosmo felt himself rise into his harness. The cockpit was degravitating!

"Brain-E and I will sort it out, Cosmo," Nuri said. "Just keep flying."

The little brainbot floated through the cabin, its scanners assessing the situation. "Acute loss of pressure," it said, pointing its probe arm to a metal panel in the ceiling.

Nuri released her harness and removed the panel, inspecting the cables and wires behind it. "The cockpit's

outer hull is cracked. We're losing cabin
pressure," she called. "Try to keep us
steady so I can fix it."

"*Steady?* You'll be lucky!" Cosmo
exclaimed, fighting to keep control in the
space storm. Lightning was flashing, and
the space winds were buffeting the
Dragster, forcing it left and right. He felt
a jolt as another asteroid clipped the
spaceship's tail, sending it spinning out
of control.

"Heeelp!" Brain-E yelped, being hurled
through the cockpit.

We can't survive much more of this, Cosmo thought desperately, accelerating to straighten his course. He glanced at a tattered photograph stuck to the control panel. It showed his dad in the cockpit of an old G-Watch Dragster 5000 – the ship he'd flown when he'd been a G-Watch agent. *What would you have done in an asteroid storm, Dad?* Cosmo wondered.

Suddenly an idea came to him. He flicked a switch on the steering column. "Engaging photon cannons," he said. "I'm going to try to *blast* our way through!"

An electronic display appeared on the spacescreen with a cross-target in its centre. As an asteroid swirled into view, he pressed a red button on the steering column, firing photon torpedoes from the cannons, smashing the asteroid to pieces.

"Good shot, Master Cosmo!" Brain-E said, floating upside down beside him.

"Go, Cosmo!" Nuri called from the back

of the cockpit. She was clinging to the ceiling, using a welding torch to seal the crack in the hull. As more deadly asteroids spun towards the Dragster, Cosmo locked them in his sights, firing again. Photon torpedoes shot from the Dragster, blasting them to pieces, while the space storm raged all around. With each shot, debris clattered the spacescreen.

"Bull's-eye!" Brain-E exclaimed, as Cosmo blasted a hole in an enormous asteroid and flew the Dragster straight through it. He fired again and again, creating a clear path. Soon he could see the end of the storm ahead. *Just keep going*, he thought. Chunks of asteroid exploded all around as Cosmo dipped and swerved.

"The hull's welded and repaired," Nuri announced from the back of the cockpit.

Cosmo glanced back and saw her sealing the last section of the crack with the welding torch. The warning light on the control desk flashed off and the alarm stopped sounding.

"Nice work, Nuri," he said, feeling himself sink back onto his seat as gravity was restored to the cabin.

"Thank goodness for that," Brain-E added, floating down to the control desk.

Cosmo felt the Dragster steadying too. The space wind outside was subsiding and the asteroids were moving more slowly. They'd made it through the space storm! He disengaged the photon cannons and glanced to the photo of his father. *We did it, Dad!* he thought.

Nuri quickly replaced the ceiling panel and returned to her seat. She tried the communicator again. "This is Agent Nuri from G-Watch. Convoy, can you hear me?"

But there was still no reply.

In the Dragster's searchlights, Cosmo saw something glistening in the distance. He slowed the ship to two vectrons and saw a white cable strung between two asteroids. Then he saw another, then another. There were hundreds of cables, criss-crossing the entire Tarn Belt. "Nuri, look! What are they?"

Nuri, Cosmo and Brain-E all peered out, astonished. The white cables were everywhere, running for miles. "It's like a huge spider's web," Brain-E exclaimed.

"Provix said Zillah used a white cable when she left *Orpheus*," Nuri remembered. "This has to be her work!"

As the Dragster's lights swept over the white web, Cosmo noticed satellites,

probes and wrecks caught in it like flies. He gasped as he spotted an enormous cargo freighter trapped among them. It was firing its thrusters, trying to break free, but it was completely stuck. "It's one of the convoy's freighters!" he cried.

Nuri spoke into the ship's communicator again. "I repeat, this is Agent Nuri of G-Watch. Can anybody hear me?"

There was a moment's silence, then a terrified voice replied over the crackle: "I can hear you. My ship's stuck!"

It was the pilot from the freighter trapped in the web!

"We've got a visual on you," Nuri told him. "We're coming to save you!"

The reply came instantly this time: "No, it's too dangerous. There's a ferocious alien around here. Save yourselves before it comes back! It's hunting us down one by one!"

CHAPTER FIVE

THE SPACE WALK

Cosmo flew the Dragster towards the trapped freighter, keeping an eye out for Zillah.

Nuri continued talking to the pilot over the crackling communicator. "What happened?" she asked.

The pilot replied in a trembling voice: "We lost contact with *Orpheus* and were buffeted by asteroids. Some of the freighters took direct hits, but we managed to stay together and made it this far. Then we got stuck in these cables. They're sticky – like glue."

"Where are the other freighters now?" Nuri asked.

"Some kind of enormous mutant spider has been taking them away, one by one. I'm the last. Get out of here while you can; it'll be back any minute."

Cosmo leaned across and spoke into the radio. "We're not going anywhere. I'm coming to get you out," he said. He unfastened his flying harness. "Nuri, take the controls. I'm going outside."

Cosmo fetched a jetpack from the kit shelves at the back of the cockpit and pushed his arms through its shoulder straps.

"Cosmo, are you crazy?" Nuri said. "You can't just stroll out for a space walk. We're in the Tarn Belt – it's not safe. The conditions here are too volatile."

Cosmo took a handheld laser cutter from the ship's toolbox and clipped it to his utility belt. "I'm going to cut the freighter free, Nuri. Watch out for Zillah."

Nuri nodded, but she looked concerned. "Cosmo, keep your helmet's communicator on, and stay close so we don't lose signal," she said.

"Sure thing," Cosmo replied, closing his visor. He stepped to the back of the cockpit and lifted the floor hatch to the airlock, then climbed inside, closing the hatch behind him. Through his earpiece he heard Nuri's voice. "Cosmo, be careful out there."

"Just keep a lookout for Zillah," Cosmo replied into his microphone. "I'll be as quick as I can." He opened the outer hatch and floated out into space.

Cosmo's body felt completely weightless. *My first ever space walk*, he thought. *I hope it's not my last*. It was freezing cold outside and ice crystals formed on his visor, but the Quantum Mutation Suit regulated his body temperature. He gripped the jetpack's joysticks and pressed its thumb buttons, igniting the jets and propelling himself towards the freighter. It was hard work.

He was being buffeted by space wind and a dark dusty space fog obscured his vision.

"Is everything OK, Cosmo?" he heard Nuri ask in his earpiece.

"Just about, though visibility's not good."

He jetted through the dark fog and brought himself down onto the huge freighter. It was dented and scraped from the asteroid impacts. He stepped over some white cables and ducked under others; then, gripping onto an antenna, he leaned down, peering into the freighter's spacescreen. "I'm going to try to cut you free," he mouthed to the pilot.

The pilot nodded, and Cosmo unclipped the laser cutter from his utility belt. He switched it on and shone its thin red laser beam onto the first cable. The cable glowed and smoked as the beam slowly sliced through it, then it pinged apart and Cosmo ducked to avoid it hitting him.

He pulled himself along the freighter's

hull, slicing one cable after another. They were each as thick as his arm and shining with sticky glue. Through the freighter's skylights he could see into its cargo hold, full of essential grain destined for the galaxy's barren planets. The hull was frosted and slippery, making it hard for him to keep his footing. The space wind was strong too, and the dusty fog was slowing him down. He worked carefully, watching out for Zillah at the same time. "Nuri, warn me if you see anything," he said.

"OK, Cosmo," Nuri replied. "But the fog's moving in. I really can't see much."

Cosmo looked over his shoulder. The dust was closing in around the web. He sped up, wanting to get back to the Dragster as fast as he could. He sliced through the last of the cables. "Nuri, I'm done," he said into his microphone. "Radio the freighter's pilot and tell him to try his thrusters at full power."

"Affirmative, Cosmo," Nuri replied. "Nice work!"

Cosmo felt the spaceship judder as its thrusters powered up. Suddenly it jerked forward and he lost his footing, slipping off its icy hull, the laser cutter falling from his hand. He grabbed the joysticks on his jetpack, firing its jets just in time to save himself from falling into the sticky web. He hovered, surrounded by the fog, and heard the freighter powering free and heading away to safety.

"Cosmo, where are you?" Nuri said.

"I'm OK, Nuri," he replied. "I'm on my way back. Tell the freighter pilot to wait for us wherever there's a break in the asteroid field."

He looked around for the Dragster, but couldn't see it. The dark fog was closing in thick and fast. "Nuri, can you turn the Dragster's lights up to maximum so I can spot you?" he asked.

"They're on full already, Cosmo," came the reply.

Cosmo tried to get his bearings, but it was confusing. Every direction looked the same – thick black fog. He could barely see more than a few metres beyond his visor. He blasted his jets, taking his best guess, but the space wind was buffeting him, disorientating him further.

Nuri's voice came over his earpiece. "Cosmo, is that you knocking on the Dragster?"

"No, Nuri, I'm not there yet. I'm still looking for you."

"Then what is it?" Nuri asked, sounding frightened.

Cosmo heard Brain-E bleeping, then saw the flashes of photon torpedoes blasting through the fog. It was the Dragster's photon cannons firing.

"Cosmo, it's Zillah!" Nuri said over the communicator. "I can't shoot her off. She's got the Dragster!"

Cosmo jetted as fast as he could in the direction of the flashes, desperate to reach Nuri. "Hold on! I'm on my way!"

But the transmission crackled and there was no reply.

"Nuri?" he called desperately. He urged on the jetpack, finally reaching the point where he'd seen the torpedo fire, but the Dragster had vanished. Zillah had snatched it, with Nuri and Brain-E on board!

CHAPTER SIX

ZILLAH'S LARDER

Meanwhile, beyond the galaxy, in a private chamber on the battleship *Oblivion*, the alien outlaw Kaos was relaxing in a huge bubble bath.

"More hot water, Wugrat!" one of Kaos's five heads ordered.

A scrawny purple rat scurried along the edge of the bath and turned a tap with its paws, releasing a gush of hot water. The room filled with steam.

"Oooh, that's better," said another of Kaos's heads. "It's so good to relax while Zillah does our dirty work!"

"When we take over the galaxy, G-Watch will be washed down the plughole," another head added, smirking.

A fourth head chuckled. "I will force their Chief, G1, to lick between our toes!" All five heads roared with laughter.

The little rat squeaked, swimming through the water with a bar of soap in its mouth.

"Clean our armpits, Wugrat!" the first head ordered it.

Kaos leaned back in the tub with his arms up, while Wugrat scrubbed. His five heads smiled cruelly.

"By now Zillah will be feasting, and the Great Western Tradeway will be closed for good," the second said.

"No ship will dare pass through the Tarn Asteroid Belt ever again, and their valuable

supplies will be stranded!" the third added.

"Soon the galaxy will be begging us for mercy."

"And G-Watch will too. Oh, I am brilliant."

"So am I!"

"And so am I!"

"And me!"

"Me too!"

***

Cosmo floated blindly through the fog. "Nuri, where are you?" he said urgently into his mic. But he could hear only a crackle.

Where has Zillah taken her? he wondered. He looked around, desperately hoping to glimpse the Dragster's lights somewhere in the fog, but he couldn't see anything. He took a deep breath to steady his nerves. *Stay calm*, he told himself. *Zillah can't have gone far. There must be a way to find her.* Inside him, Cosmo felt his power surge and the Quantum Mutation Suit began to glow. He told himself to be brave. *I can do this. I have to.*

He thought hard. *The answer must be in the web*, he decided. Its white threads, barely visible in the fog, stretched among the asteroids for miles in all directions. An idea came to him. *Even if I can't see the fanged predator, perhaps I can feel which way she went.* He jetted among the cables, touching them gently with the back of his gloved hands, being sure not to grip them and get stuck. He worked his way gradually from cable to cable, feeling each one in turn. At last he found what he was feeling for: faint pinging vibrations, as if somewhere far along the cable, something was walking along it.

Zillah! he thought triumphantly.

He jetted off as fast as he could, following the cable, on the trail of the invader. It led him to a huge asteroid, a broken chunk of a black planet. *So this is where Zillah took them*, he thought, and he descended onto it and switched off his jetpack. He looked around nervously in the darkness. *Zillah could be hiding, waiting to strike*. He heard a noise behind him and spun round, his heart thumping.

"Master Cosmo, am I glad to see you!"

He looked down and saw Brain-E scuttling towards him.

"Brain-E, you're safe!" Cosmo said, bending down and picking up the little brainbot. "What happened? Is Nuri OK?"

"Zillah has the Dragster, Master. I escaped through the waste vent to look for you, but Mistress Nuri is still trapped!"

"Where is she now, Brain-E? Show me."

The little robot pointed a quivering metal leg towards the entrance to a huge dark cave. "In there."

Cosmo hurried to the cave, bounding with long strides in the asteroid's weak gravity.

"We must be quiet, Master Cosmo," Brain-E whispered, heading inside.

The cave was over a hundred metres high, and in its vast dark chamber Cosmo could make out cables criss-crossing from one wall to the other. Overhead he saw faint glowing lights coming from enormous white cocoons suspended from the cave's roof. Suddenly he realized that they were the headlights of spaceships. They were the convoy's freighters, each bound in sticky thread.

Brain-E bleeped. "The alien has captured the freighters and appears to be storing them, Master Cosmo," it whispered.

"Storing them? What for?"

"This place is its larder. It's preparing a feast."

Cosmo clambered between the sticky threads, looking up in horror. He counted seven large freighters, each hanging in a cocoon, plus a smaller one – the Dragster 7000!

"Nuri's up there, trapped inside it," Brain-E said. "She can't get out."

Cosmo whispered into his mic. "Nuri, can you hear me?"

He heard a crackle, then a faint voice: "Cosmo, is that you?"

"Nuri, I can see where you are. I'm coming to save you!"

But then he heard something moving in the shadows above. *Tap tap tap . . . tap tap*

tap . . . It sounded like daggers on rock.

Shivers ran down Cosmo's spine.

"Zillah's up there too, Master Cosmo," Brain-E whispered.

At that moment Cosmo saw an enormous alien leap from the shadows onto one of the cocooned freighters and plunge two long, sharp fangs into it, oozing green slime. *She's liquefying the freighters to feed on them!* Cosmo realized. *And the pilots are still inside!*

Cosmo set his jetpack on the ground by the little robot. "Keep back, Brain-E, and look after this," he said.

"Don't you need it, Master Cosmo?"

Cosmo took a deep breath. "No. It's time to use the Quantum Mutation Suit."

CHAPTER SEVEN

SCREELON

Cosmo felt a brave energy welling inside him and the Quantum Mutation Suit began pulsing with light. It was activating. "SCAN," he said into the helmet's voice sensor. The Quantum Mutation Suit scanned through its databank. On the visor's digital display, images of aliens appeared one after another, along with vital statistics on each. Cosmo saw a fire-breathing rebos, a sting-tailed oklo, a spiral-horned decimon. *What could beat Zillah?* he thought. On the display he saw a bat-like alien with sharp talons and leathery wings.

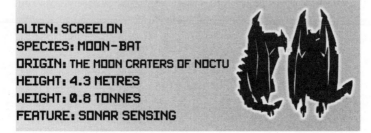

ALIEN: SCREELON
SPECIES: MOON-BAT
ORIGIN: THE MOON CRATERS OF NOCTU
HEIGHT: 4.3 METRES
WEIGHT: 0.8 TONNES
FEATURE: SONAR SENSING

Sonar sensing! That means it can see in the dark, Cosmo thought. *Perfect! Let's see how Zillah deals with Screelon!*

"MUTATE," he said into the helmet's voice sensor. His body tingled as the Quantum Mutation Suit fused with his skin. He could feel the molecules inside him reconfiguring. His finger bones lengthened until they touched the ground, and his skin stretched between them, forming large leathery wings. Razor-sharp talons sprouted from his wingtips and his legs became hairy. His body grew until he was

over four metres tall, with long ears that
could pick up the smallest sounds.

He let out an ultrasonic screech that
bounced around the cave. His sonar
sensing picked up the pattern of the
sound waves and formed a picture in his
mind of the cave's interior – he was using
his ears as eyes!

High above in the darkness he saw
Zillah hanging from one of the freighters
like a giant skeletal spider. She had eight
long limbs, as sharp as spears, and was

gripping the cocooned freighter. Her mouth was open, baring sharp fangs, ready to bite into it. Her black glassy eyes swivelled downwards, glaring at him.

"In the name of G-Watch, I order you to stop!" Cosmo shouted.

"I only take ordersss from Kaossss," Zillah hissed.

"Then prepare to be squashed, you overgrown bug!" Cosmo flapped his enormous leathery wings and soared up into the darkness, weaving between the white cables. With his long talons outstretched he let out a screech, pinpointing the alien with his sonar. He struck Zillah, tearing her off the cocooned freighter and hurling her across the cavern. "Take that, Spidey!"

Zillah's eight spear-like limbs kicked and struggled as she tumbled downwards into the mass of white threads. "Aargh!"

Cosmo landed on the cocooned freighter

and, with his sharp talons, slashed the threads encasing it, revealing the freighter's cockpit door. The door fell open and he pulled the pilot out.

"Th-th-thanks," the pilot said. "Whatever you are."

Cosmo swooped down carrying him, dropping him beside Brain-E. "Stay hidden," he said.

"You don't really think you can defeat me, do you?" Zillah's shrill voice echoed around the cavern.

Cosmo let out a screech, and with his sonar sensing he detected the invader scuttling up the wall, heading for the other cocooned ships. He flexed his wings and flew after her. But as he attacked she stuck out a sharp leg, ripping his wing. Cosmo flapped around in pain.

"I will eat you for my sssupper," Zillah hissed angrily.

Cosmo swooped again, gripping hold of

her spidery leg with his talons and swinging the invader across the cave. Zillah saved herself by shooting out a sticky thread and pulling herself up to the ceiling.

She hid in the dark, and Cosmo let out another ultrasonic screech, trying to detect her.

"I'm right above you!" she hissed.

Suddenly a thick white thread shot down and lassoed Cosmo, clamping his wings to his sides. He felt himself being hoisted up and rolled over and over, as the invader bound him with the sticky thread. Cosmo struggled to free himself, trying to tear his way out with his claws, but it was no use: he was wrapped too tightly to move, a strong cocoon forming around him.

"Let me go!" he ordered.

Zillah let out a hideous hissing laugh. "Never! I shall ssssave you for dessssert."

The invader suspended him by a thread from the roof of the cavern alongside the freighters.

Cosmo couldn't move a muscle. "RESET," he said, changing from his moon-bat form back to his boy self. Smaller now, he had more room to move inside the cocoon. But there was still no way out – he was trapped.

CHAPTER EIGHT

LASER EYES

Cosmo punched at the walls of the cocoon, trying to force his way out, but he couldn't break free. He tried to push his hands between the threads but they were stuck tightly together. From outside the cocoon he could hear the slurping sound of Zillah feeding on the melted freighter. *If only I had the laser cutter now*, he thought. *I could cut myself free*. He wished he hadn't dropped it in the fog.

"SCAN," Cosmo said into his helmet's voice sensor. Images of aliens began appearing in front of his eyes as, once again, the Quantum Mutation Suit scrolled through its databank. *I need an alien that can get me out of here and smash that overgrown mutant spider*, he thought. He checked out a gore-horned thoedos, a spring-heeled katsu and an armour-plated voston. Then he saw a tall, muscular alien with glowing red eyes:

ALIEN: LASARG
SPECIES: ARGONITE
ORIGIN: PLANET KOVAR
HEIGHT: 7.1 METRES
WEIGHT: 1.3 TONNES
FEATURE: LASER-EYES

Lasarg's laser-eyes should do it!

"MUTATE!" Cosmo said. He felt a rush of energy as, once more, the Quantum Mutation Suit reconfigured the molecules of his body. He grew taller, his limbs enlarging and his muscles bulging, stretching the cocoon. He could feel his eyes heating up, shining bright red. Lasers shot from them, burning clean through the cocoon's threads and splitting it open. Cosmo jumped out and tumbled down a sticky cable, landing on the ground.

He looked up at Zillah, who was still feeding. "Dinner time's over, Zillah!" he shouted, fixing her in his laser sights. His eyes felt a surge of heat and he shot two laser beams from them, blasting the invader.

"Aargh!" Zillah shrieked, tumbling down among the threads. "You again! You're giving me indigessstion."

Cosmo shot two more laser beams, but the invader leaped away into the shadows and they blasted the rock wall with a red flash.

"I warn you. Do not messsss with me," Zillah hissed.

But as Lasarg, Cosmo felt strong. "Come out and fight!" he called.

A thread shot at him, binding his legs together, but Cosmo simply sliced through it with his laser eyes. "It's no use, Zillah! You're history!"

Seeing where the thread had come from, he fired his laser eyes again. In a flash of red he saw Zillah leap upwards, shooting another thread to the roof and scuttling away up it. With another blast of his laser beams, Cosmo severed the thread and sent Zillah crashing back to the cavern floor. *Zap!* Another blast sent her scuttling away to the back of the cavern. *I'm winning!* Cosmo thought excitedly.

He stared into the darkness, listening for the sound of Zillah's spear-like legs. "Come out and fight, I said!"

"Tsssssss, tsssss, tsssss."

Cosmo heard Zillah's laughter echo through the cave. Then he heard the clang of metal and looked up. Zillah had tricked him! She was back up among the cocoons, sinking her fangs into another of the freighters, injecting it with her digestive saliva. Cosmo blasted his lasers, but this time the invader leaped to the next cocoon, narrowly avoiding them. There came a second clang as her fangs punctured another freighter's hull. Cosmo fired again and again, but Zillah was nimble, leaping and swinging on threads, injecting the freighters one after the other. *Clang!* her fangs went. *Clang! Clang!*

I have to get the pilots out, Cosmo thought. He focused his laser eyes on one of the cocooned freighters and fired the beams down its side, splitting the cocoon open. The pilot leaped from the freighter's cockpit door wearing a breathing sphere, and tumbled down through the cables. Cosmo directed his lasers at the next ship, freeing another

pilot. One by one, he split open each of
the cocoons, and the pilots tumbled down
the threads to safety.

As he freed the last pilot, he heard
bleeping. "Master, quickly – up here!"

Brain-E had climbed up a cable and was clinging to the cocooned Dragster, flashing its lights in panic.

Cosmo saw the little brainbot bravely trying to fight Zillah, poking her with its radio antenna. But with one flick of her hairy leg, Zillah sent Brain-E spinning.

"Heeeeeeeeeeeelp!" Brain-E called.

Cosmo reached out his huge hand and caught the little brainbot. He looked up at Zillah – the alien had latched herself onto the cocooned Dragster! "Hey, my friend's in that ship!" He shot two powerful laser beams at the fanged invader, blasting her off the cocoon.

"Cursssses!" Zillah crashed down and scuttled away into the shadows. Cosmo fired again, cutting the Dragster's cocoon. Its cockpit door opened and Nuri jumped out, falling down through the cables.

"Thank you, Cosmo!" she gasped, landing beside him.

"Nuri, look after Brain-E and the
pilots," Cosmo said, handing her the
brainbot. "I'm going after Zillah!"

He cut his way through the sticky
threads, heading deeper into the cavern
in pursuit of the alien invader.

Away from the lights of the spaceships,
it was even darker still. Cosmo shone
his laser eyes to the back of the cavern
and saw an opening to a second chamber.

He heard scuttling from inside and fired two laser beams in the direction of the sound. The lasers struck the rock walls and the chamber lit up briefly. Cosmo saw boulders strewn across the ground and Zillah leaping aside.

He strode into the dark chamber to blast her again, but as he did a boulder swung down on a thread and struck his back.

"Oof!" Cosmo fell to his knees. Another boulder swung towards him and hit him on the shoulder. "Ouch!"

"It'ssss my turn to get you now," he heard from above.

Cosmo looked up, letting out blasts with his laser eyes. The chamber flashed as laser beams ricocheted off its walls, but the invader had vanished again. She was *fast*.

"Can't you ssssee me?" It was Zillah's voice, speaking in a mocking whisper. "Too quick for you, am I?"

Cosmo couldn't see the alien in the dark, but he realized that she could still see him. At that moment, another boulder shot through the darkness and struck Cosmo straight in the face. He felt a shooting pain in his head and his eyes blurred. Dizzy, he fell to the ground.

CHAPTER NINE

A LIGHT IN THE DARK

Cosmo crawled across the cold, damp ground, shaken by the force of the boulder. His head was throbbing with pain and his laser eyes fizzed. He had to summon all his strength just to stay conscious. "RESET," he said, and he changed back into his boy self.

He scrambled towards the chamber entrance to take cover and saw a tiny speck of light. It was Nuri, shining a torch from the main cavern.

"Are you OK, Cosmo?" she called.

But as he crawled towards her, he heard a loud scraping sound. A large boulder was rolling across the entrance, sealing him in! *I'm trapped*, he thought desperately.

"We're alone now," he heard Zillah hiss menacingly. "Alone in the dark."

It was pitch black now. Cosmo could hear himself breathing and Zillah tapping her spear legs on the wall of the cave. He listened carefully: her sounds seemed to be coming from his left. Or was it his right? It was impossible to tell where the invader was.

"What'sss wrong? Isss the brave G-Watch agent afraid of the dark?" Zillah taunted.

Cosmo felt vulnerable. The alien was watching him in the darkness with her big black eyes, taunting him, preparing to strike! *Think*, he said to himself. *There must be a way to win . . .*

"SCAN," he said into the sensor of the Quantum Mutation Suit. On its visor's digital display, images of aliens appeared once again. He spotted a tiny alien that blazed like a bright white light.

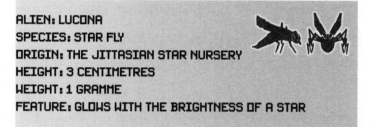

ALIEN: LUCONA
SPECIES: STAR FLY
ORIGIN: THE JITTASIAN STAR NURSERY
HEIGHT: 3 CENTIMETRES
WEIGHT: 1 GRAMME
FEATURE: GLOWS WITH THE BRIGHTNESS OF A STAR

A star fly! Cosmo had an idea. *Zillah's eyes must be sensitive if she can see in the dark,* he thought. *Let's see how she sees in the light!* "MUTATE."

Instantly, he felt himself changing for a third time. He began shrinking, smaller and smaller, until he was the size of a fly. His skin turned pearly-white and his arms became thin, delicate wings. His eyes bulged and his vision altered, seeing everything in tiny multi-coloured dots. He was a minuscule star fly, and started to glow. In his light, he saw Zillah move above him on the ceiling, her fangs bared, a spear-like leg outstretched.

"Your magic won't sssave you now!" she hissed. "I'll gobble you up, little fly!"

In a burst of light, Cosmo radiated a bright flash as strong and powerful as a burning star. As Lucona, he was blinding.

"Aarrrrgh!" Zillah shrieked, trying to shield her eyes. She fell from the ceiling, curling up into a ball and wailing in the glare of the light.

"And now to finish you!" Cosmo said.

He spoke the command, "RESET," and his fly-like body tingled as he turned back into a boy.

"Never!" the invader shrieked. She lay blinded on the ground, spitting green saliva from her mouth. Her long limbs jabbed like spears as she tried to get to her feet.

Cosmo summoned all the power inside him, and the Quantum Mutation Suit began to glow. From the pit of his stomach, then along his arm, he felt his power surge. It felt almost electric. His gloved hand tingled as a bright, sword-like light extended from it like a bolt of lightning. "The power of the universe is in me!" he said. He raised the power sword and charged at Zillah, plunging it into her.

The invader screeched: "NOOOO!"

Cosmo felt his whole body vibrate, his power locked in battle with Zillah's hideous greed. Every molecule in his body was fighting with hers. He saw her glassy eyes turn red and bloodshot. Her limbs twitched and her body crumpled, screwing up into a writhing mass. She let out a long, trailing 'hissssssss' then a fading screech as she exploded into a million pieces – a cloud of black dust.

Cosmo sank to his knees, exhausted. The cave was pitch dark once more, but Zillah had been defeated and his ordeal was at an end. He heard the scraping sound of rock and turned, seeing a chink of light appear at the entrance to the cave.

"That's it, men. One last heave . . ."

It was Nuri with the freighter pilots! They were pushing the huge boulder away from the entrance. "Heave!"

It rolled to one side, and Cosmo blinked in the light from Nuri's torch. "You did it, Cosmo! You're alive!"

"Just about," Cosmo replied with a smile. "And Zillah's gone for good."

One of the pilots nervously poked his head in. "You fought that alien?" he asked in amazement. "By yourself?"

"You're all safe now," Cosmo said. "Zillah won't be troubling you any more."

***

Meanwhile, back on the battleship *Oblivion*, Kaos woke with a splutter. He had fallen asleep in the bath. The water was cold, and all the bubbles had disappeared. Worse still, he could hear Wugrat squeaking at him shrilly from the doorway.

"What is it, Wugrat?" Kaos's first head spat.

The purple wugrat scurried over to the bath and squeaked again, all in a fluster.

"What? Zillah's navicom signal has vanished?" Kaos's second head asked. "But that means—"

Kaos slammed his fist into the cold bath water, seething with rage. "Stinking starbursts! Zillah has been defeated!"

"How could this happen?" his third head fumed.

"G-Watch must have some secret weapon."

"Well, it won't work next time. Wugrat, fetch another navicom! We shall send in Hydronix."

"Yes! Hydronix!"

"Hydronix!"

"Hydronix!"

Kaos leaped out of the bath, drenching Wugrat, and threw on his bathrobe. He

swept down the corridors of *Oblivion*
into its cargo hold. Inside stood two more
enormous aliens: one with long, thick
tentacles and the other glowing green.

"Hydronix, you're up next!"

Wugrat skittered over with a crystal
navicom transporter disc in his mouth.

Kaos snatched it from him, turned its outer ring to set its coordinates, then fastened it to one of Hydronix's tentacles.

"MY TURN TO INVADE!" Hydronix bellowed.

The huge alien stomped to the middle

of the cargo hold and looked up as the ceiling opened, revealing the swirling stars of the Doom Vortex. The navicom started to flash and a blue light radiated from it. With a *whoosh*, Hydronix shot out of the battleship.

CHAPTER TEN

A NEW ADVENTURE

Cosmo flew the Dragster back through the
Tarn Belt, weaving between asteroids.
The freighter pilots had helped him and
Nuri free his spaceship from its cocoon,
and they were all on board. Flying behind
the Dragster was the freighter that
Cosmo had freed from Zillah's web
earlier. In the absence of *Orpheus*'s
remote guidance he was leading it to
safety. The way out of the Tarn Belt was

still hazardous, with a space blizzard and a fierce comet shower to negotiate, but Cosmo flew skillfully and at last they emerged, exhausted but triumphant. The Dragster locked onto the freighter and all the pilots transferred safely aboard. They waved as the freighter flew off along the tradeway.

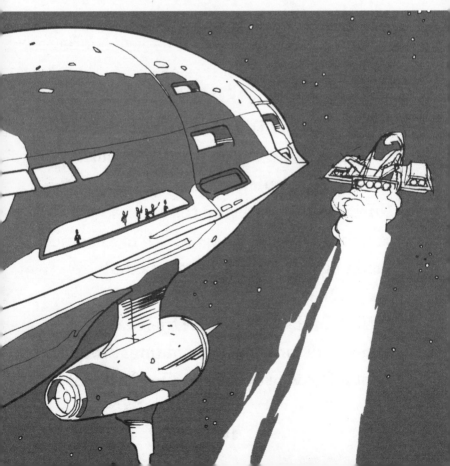

With the airwaves clear, Nuri switched
on the Dragster's communicator to contact
G-Watch headquarters. The monitor
flickered and G1's face appeared. "What's
the news?" he asked anxiously.

"Mission accomplished, G1," Cosmo
said. "Zillah is terminated."

The silver-eyed Chief of G-Watch smiled
with relief. "Congratulations," he said.

"Engineers are needed at space station
Orpheus," Nuri said. "It needs rebuilding."

"G-Watch agents will get straight onto
it," G1 replied. "The Great Western
Tradeway will soon re-open to space
traffic, thanks to you."

Cosmo and Nuri glanced at one
another and smiled.

"Good job, team," Brain-E said, its
lights flashing happily.

G1 coughed, as if to get their attention.
"I'm afraid the galaxy is not totally safe
yet, though," he said. "Kaos has already

dispatched his fourth invader. Our scanners have detected it heading for the holiday planet of Oceania in the Gamma Quadrant. We believe it to be Hydronix, destroyer of the deep."

Cosmo readied the Dragster's thrusters. "We'll go after it, Chief. Right away."

"Good luck," G1 replied. "The power of the universe is in you!"

The screen flickered and the transmission ended. Cosmo checked the controls, then blasted away from the Tarn Belt. "Nuri, set a course for Planet Oceania. Let's go get Hydronix!"

Join Cosmo on his next **ALIEN INVADERS**
mission. He must face – and defeat

HYDRONIX

DESTROYER OF THE DEEP

INVADER ALERT!

"Mum, please can I have a go on the robo-bungee?" Jako asked.

Jako's mother was sunbathing in front of the beach hotel, tanning her yellow Utraxian skin. She opened her three eyes and smiled at him. "Of course you can."

"Brilliant!" Jako raced away, his tail swishing along the red sand. *Robo-bungee, here I come!*

Jako and his mother were holidaying on Oceania, a water planet with nineteen artificial islands, a sparkling golden ocean and coral reefs. He ran down the beach, weaving between holidaymakers – more were out snorkelling, turbo-sailing and propeller-boarding. He stopped beside a thirty-metre-tall robot. Its huge metal hand was bouncing a frog-headed Mervish boy up and down into the water on an elastic bungee rope.

"Me next, please!" Jako called up.

The robo-bungee placed the grinning wet Mervish boy on the sand, then lifted Jako high into the air until he could see brightly coloured corals, shoals of fish – even some jumbola whales.

"Bungee attaching," the robot said, clamping the bungee rope around Jako's ankles. *"Ten . . . nine . . . eight . . ."*

Here I go! Jako thought excitedly. But just as he was readying himself to dive, he heard a sound like thunder and saw something hurtling down through the mauve sky. It hit the water about a mile away, sending up a plume of spray. A large dark shape moved towards the island.

". . . three. . . two . . . one . . . Bungee!"

The robot sent Jako diving headfirst. As he plunged into the water, he glimpsed fish and corals and—

Jako gasped. Swimming towards the island was a terrifying alien with a barnacled face and enormous grasping tentacles! Suddenly the bungee rope pinged him back up into the air. He called out in panic: "There's a monster down there!"

Jako's stomach lurched as he dived into the water again. This time he saw the alien's huge tentacles curling around the island's flotation cylinders, trying to rip them free. He felt the bungee rope tighten, and it shot him back up. The whole island was rocking, the robo-bungee swinging him sideways with it.

"Help!" Jako called out. "There's a monster attacking the island!"

The hotel began to sway. Holidaymakers were screaming.

"Mum, help!" Jako called, bouncing helplessly up and down on the rope. He watched in terror as a tentacle reached up out of the water and smashed a hole through the wall of the hotel. Another slammed down onto the beach, opening up a wide crack.

"The island's breaking up!" someone shouted. "Everyone off!"

"Robo-bungee, I want to get down!" Jako cried.

One of the alien's tentacles whacked the robo-bungee, toppling it into the ocean with Jako still attached. He gasped as he was pulled under the water, the weight of the sinking metal robot tugging on the bungee rope. He plummeted past the terrifying tentacled alien and heard it bellow: "I am Hydronix and, by order of Kaos, I have come to DESTROY!"

CHAPTER ONE
DESTINATION: OCEANIA

Cosmo heard a computerized voice speaking in his ear: *"Sleep acceleration complete. On the count of three, open your eyes. One . . . two . . . three . . ."*

He opened his eyes, feeling bright and alert. He was lying on the rest bunk in the cockpit of the Dragster 7000, wearing a sleep-acceleration headset. His co-pilot, Agent Nuri, a blue-skinned girl from the planet Etrusia, was at the controls.

"How long was I asleep for?" he asked.

"Only ten Earth minutes," Nuri replied.

"That's amazing! I feel like I've been asleep for hours."

"The sleep accelerator provides one hour's sleep for every minute. It works on your central nervous system. It should have replenished your energy for the battle ahead."

I could do with a sleep accelerator back on Earth when I'm too tired to get up for school, Cosmo thought with a grin.

Cosmo Santos was an eleven-year-old Earthling boy on a mission for the galaxy's security force, G-Watch, to save the galaxy from five alien invaders. They were being beamed in by the galactic outlaw Kaos, using navicom transporter devices. So far Cosmo had defeated three of them: Rockhead, the living mountain; Infernox, the firestarter; and Zillah, the fanged predator. Now he was heading for the holiday planet Oceania to face the fourth invader, the underwater alien, Hydronix.

"How long until we're due to arrive, Nuri?" he asked, lifting off the headset.

"About eight minutes," Nuri replied. "Take the controls again while I check the kit."

Cosmo jumped into the pilot's seat. It was good to be back at the controls. The Dragster was leaving the galaxy's Great Western Tradeway, heading south. He tapped the spacescreen, activating its star plotter, and words lit up on the glass:

DESTINATION: PLANET OCEANIA
STAR SYSTEM: GREKKOX-2
ROUTE: SOUTH FROM GREAT WESTERN TRADEWAY
DISTANCE: 1.5 MILLION MILES

The spacescreen turned a bright flaming green as the Dragster flew through the trail of a comet. Cosmo turned the steering column and accelerated out of it, heading south towards Grekkox-2.

"Nuri, have you ever been to Oceania before?" he asked, tapping the spacescreen to deactivate the plotter.

"I once spent a week there, reef diving off Zeta Island," she replied from the back of the cockpit. "The ocean's an incredible golden colour and the corals are amazing."

Cosmo loved scuba diving. His dad, who'd been a G-Watch agent himself, had taught him one summer holiday back on Earth.

From the Dragster's control desk, the ship's bug-like brainbot, Brain-E, bleeped. "On Oceania there are nineteen holiday islands and all kinds of activities to enjoy: scuba diving, submarine rides, robo-bungee, propeller-boarding—"

"Brain-E, I don't think this mission is going to be a holiday for us," Nuri laughed. "We're going there to fight an alien invader, remember."

The brainbot flashed its lights nervously.

"Don't worry, I'll look after you," Cosmo told it kindly.

Cosmo had been recruited to G-Watch

because of a power he possessed inside – the power of the universe – which was present in all living things, but uniquely strong in him. It gave him courage and a superhuman energy within.

The Dragster flew into Grekkox-2, and Cosmo saw a huge golden planet orbiting a red star. He recognized it from galacto-vision holiday commercials he'd seen back on Earth. "Oceania is straight ahead, Nuri," he said. "Prepare for entry."

Nuri jumped back into the co-pilot's seat and buckled up.

The Dragster shook as it cut through Planet Oceania's atmosphere into a beautiful mauve sky. They flew down through wispy clouds until, far below, Cosmo saw the ocean. It stretched out in all directions, glittering in the sunlight.

"Wow!" he said. "The ocean really *is* golden here."

"There are microscopic gold-coloured plankton that live in the water," Nuri explained. "They're what the corals and the sea life feed on."

Cosmo could make out brightly coloured reefs: red, yellow and electric-blue. He saw shoals of alien fish swimming among them, and huge green whales spouting water.

"Look at the size of those whales!" he said.

Brain-E extended its stalk eyes, peering down through the spacescreen. "That's a jumbola whale, Master Cosmo, a protected species."

Nuri checked the navigation console. "Keep your eyes peeled, team. According to G-Watch's scanners, Hydronix will have struck somewhere around here."

Cosmo looked out for signs of the invader. "Brain-E, what do we know about this alien?" he asked.

"My databank states that Hydronix originates from the Whirlpools of Vahl in the Doom Vortex. He is a barnacled alien of the deep, with enormous tentacles that are strong enough to crush rock."

Cosmo gulped. *That's all I need!*

"Look – there are the islands," Nuri said.

Cosmo flew over the first and second islands, looking down at holidaymakers on the beaches and in the water. But as the Dragster neared the third, he realized something was wrong. Spaceships were taking off, whizzing up into the sky. "Everyone's leaving," he said. Pieces of broken island were jutting from the ocean like icebergs. People were frantically swimming out to boats.

Cosmo slowed the Dragster and circled overhead. The island had split into chunks, with a hotel on one and sections of beach on the others. Its flotation cylinders were deflating, bubbling in the water, and the chunks were slowly sinking.

"Hydronix must have struck here!" Cosmo said, alarmed.

There was no one left on the broken island apart from one yellow-skinned Utraxian woman clinging to a palm tree on the sloping beach. She waved her arms hysterically, calling out.

"If the island sinks, that woman will be sucked down with it!" Nuri said.

"We have to rescue her," Cosmo replied. He checked the planet's environment:

PLENTIFUL OXYGEN ... TEMPERATURE TWENTY-NINE DEGREES CENTIGRADE ... GRAVITY NORMAL.

The Dragster was now hovering above the woman. "Nuri, take the controls," he said.

Nuri took over and Cosmo headed for the kit shelves at the back of the cockpit. "What are you going to do?" she asked.

Cosmo slipped a harness over his body, then attached it to the Dragster's winch cable. "I'm going down to get her."

Find out what happens in
HYDRONIX – DESTROYER OF THE DEEP . . .